# Follow
# the Line
## around the world

words and art by

## Laura
## Ljungkvist

VIKING

-09

Follow the line
and take a trip.
We can travel by bus,
helicopter, or ship.

Along the way,
who knows what we'll see.
All kinds of animals
roam proud and free.

Some might be big, and some might be small.
Some might be short, and some might be tall.

Let's sail 'round the world in a giant balloon.
We'll stop off in Russia—and even the moon!

Turn the page and feel the hot sun in . . .

# Kenya.

Kenya is a country located in Africa.

Female elephants and their babies live together in herds.
Male elephants usually live alone.

Within a few hours of being born,
a baby giraffe can run around.

Cheetahs are the fastest land animals        on earth.

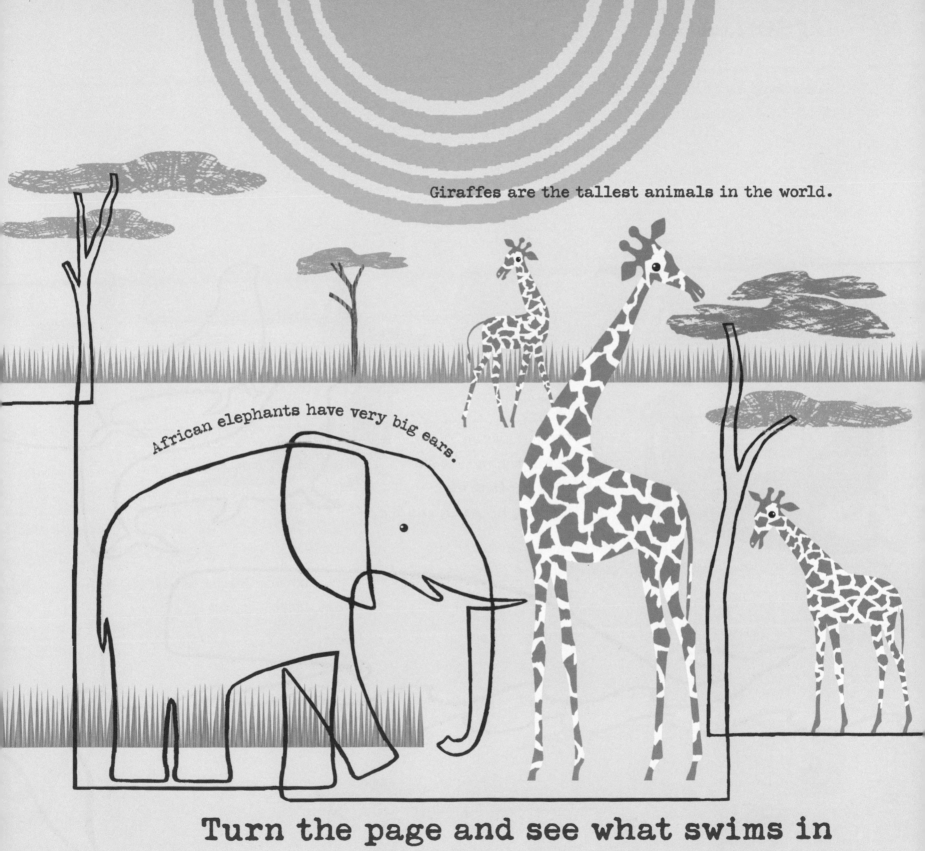

Giraffes are the tallest animals in the world.

African elephants have very big ears.

Turn the page and see what swims in
the waters off . . .

# Greenland.

Greenland is part of North America but belongs to Denmark.

Walruses use
their tusks
for fighting and
making holes in the ice.

Some whales can live to be 100 years old.

Under its white fur, a polar bear has black skin.

Greenland is not very green. It is mostly covered with snow and ice.

The blue whale is the largest animal that has ever lived.

Turn the page and warm up in . . .

# the Sahara Desert.

The Sahara Desert, located in Africa, is the largest hot desert in the world. It is almost as big as the entire United States.

A camel can go for 17 days without drinking water.

Camels have very long eyelashes to protect their eyes from blowing sand.

Cobras are deaf, so they must depend on their other senses.

It hardly ever rains in the Sahara Desert,
one of the hottest places on earth.

Ancient
Egyptians built
the pyramids
thousands of years
ago as burial grounds
for their royalty.

Camels have
big padded feet to help
them walk on the soft, hot sand.

Turn the page and see what grows in ...

# the Amazon Rainforest.

The Amazon Rainforest includes parts of eight
South American countries and one French territory.

Hundreds of kinds
of butterflies
live here.

Anacondas are among the longest snakes in the world.

Many types of medicines come from plants that grow in the Amazon Rainforest.

Parrots can live to be 100 years old.

Macaw parrots usually mate for life.

The jaguar is a powerful hunter—no other animal in the jungle can win a fight against it.

# Turn the page and go to the beach in . . .

# Sri Lanka.

Sri Lanka is an island in South Asia shaped like a teardrop.

Indian elephants have smaller ears than African elephants.

Sea turtles can live to be over 80 years old.

The first palm trees grew around 80 million years ago.

Most elephants sleep during the day,
when it is too hot to roam around.

Female sea turtles lay their eggs on the beach at night, then go back to sea.

Turn the page and dry off in . . .

# Mexico.

Mexico is a country in North America.

Some cacti bloom with colorful flowers after a rainfall.

Javelinas live in family groups.

Some tortoises have lived longer than 150 years.

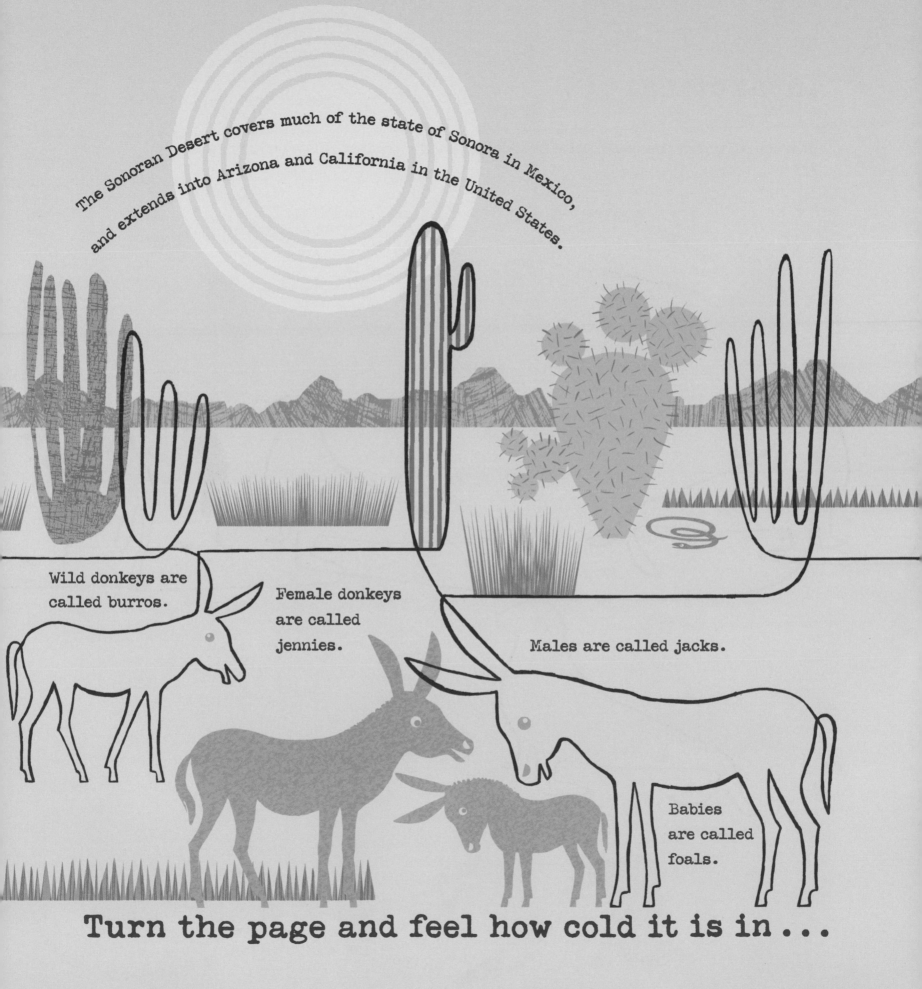

The Sonoran Desert covers much of the state of Sonora in Mexico, and extends into Arizona and California in the United States.

Wild donkeys are called burros.

Female donkeys are called jennies.

Males are called jacks.

Babies are called foals.

Turn the page and feel how cold it is in . . .

# Antarctica.

Antarctica, where the South Pole is located, is the coldest place on earth.

Few kinds of animals—and no people—live in and around Antarctica.

Fur seals use their flippers to move in the sea and on land.

Whales are mammals, so they rise to the surface of the water to breathe.

Antarctica is a frozen desert where it almost never rains or snows.

Penguins can't fly, but they are really good swimmers and can stay underwater for a long time.

# Turn the page and see if it's snowing in ...

# the Russian taiga.

The taiga covers many regions, including northern Canada, Scandinavia, and a large part of Russia. "Taiga" is the Russian word for a swampy forest.

The male moose, called a bull, has antlers; the female does not.

A taiga is an evergreen forest with very harsh winters and warm, humid summers.

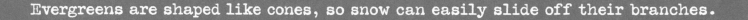
Evergreens are shaped like cones, so snow can easily slide off their branches.

For half the year it can be very dark in the taiga, because the sun does not rise high in the sky.

Deer are excellent swimmers.

Some black bears sleep—or hibernate— for up to five months in the winter.

# Turn the page and visit the Outback in . . .

# Australia.

Australia is a country and also the smallest continent.

A baby kangaroo stays in its mother's pouch all the time for its first seven months.

Female kangaroos are called does, males are called bucks, and babies are called joeys.

Australia's big desert wilderness is called the Outback.

The wild dogs in Australia are called dingoes.

Bilbies are small furry animals that are almost blind, but they can hear and smell very well.

Emus can't fly, but they can run very fast.

Turn the page and see the skyline in . . .

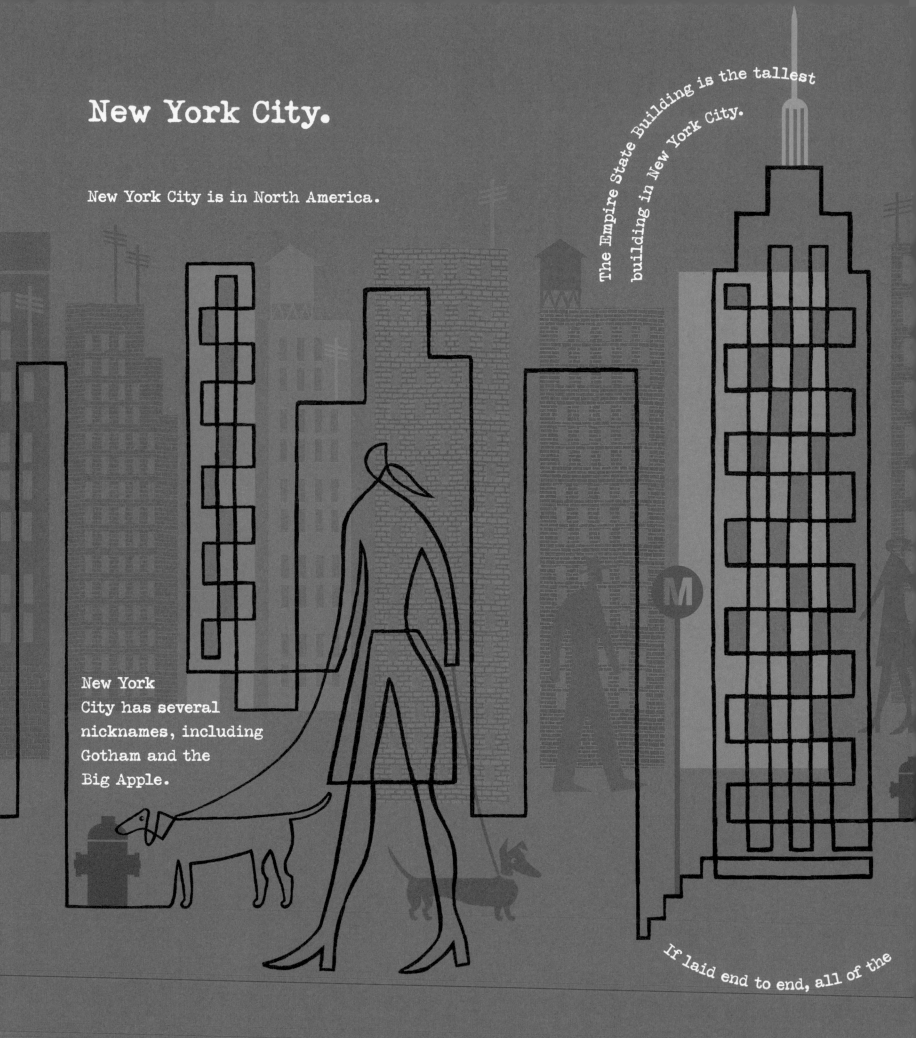

# New York City.

New York City is in North America.

The Empire State Building is the tallest building in New York City.

New York City has several nicknames, including Gotham and the Big Apple.

If laid end to end, all of the

More people live in New York City than in any other city in the United States.

Nearly 170 different languages are spoken in New York City.

The Statue of Liberty was a gift from France in 1886.

subway tracks in New York City would stretch from the city to Chicago.

# Turn the page and count the stars in . . .

# Space.

Planet Earth spins around the sun together with seven other planets. This is called a solar system.

Satellites send pictures and data back to earth.

Saturn's rings are made mostly of ice.

There are too many stars in the universe to count.

Pluto used to be considered a planet, but now it's not.

No one knows how big the universe is.

The sun is the largest object in our solar system.

No one knows if there is life on any other planet except Earth.

Turn the page and see . . .

# the whole world!

New York City

Mexico

Amazon

Planet Earth is in our care.

It is a home that we all share.

Help save animals and keep the air clean,

the water pure, and the forests green.

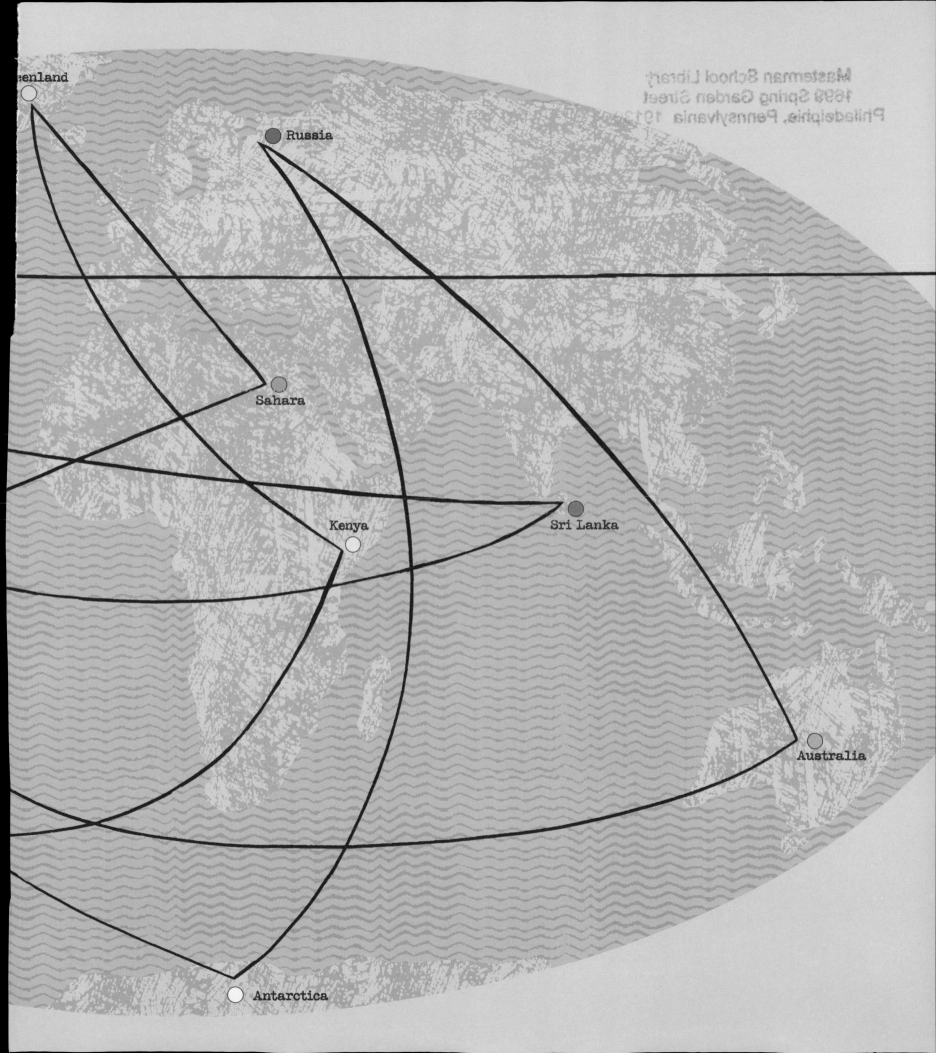

eenland

Russia

Sahara

Kenya

Sri Lanka

Australia

Antarctica

● Space

For my daughter, Violet,
in hopes that this will all be here
for you to experience.

Thanks to my husband for his help
and support while I was making this book.

Thanks to Team Viking and to the knowledgeable nature
enthusiasts all over the world who enabled me to travel
the globe without leaving my Brooklyn studio by
creating fun, interesting, informative Web sites!

—L.L.

VIKING
Published by Penguin Group
Penguin Young Readers Group, 345 Hudson Street, New York, New York 10014, U.S.A.
Penguin Group (Canada), 90 Eglinton Avenue East, Suite 700, Toronto, Ontario, Canada M4P 2Y3 (a division of Pearson Penguin Canada Inc.)
Penguin Books Ltd, Registered Offices: 80 Strand, London WC2R 0RL, England
First published in 2008 by Viking, a division of Penguin Young Readers Group

1 3 5 7 9 10 8 6 4 2

Copyright © Laura Ljungkvist, 2008
All rights reserved

LIBRARY OF CONGRESS CATALOGING—IN—PUBLICATION DATA
Ljungkvist, Laura.
Follow the line around the world / words and art by Laura Ljungkvist.
p. cm.
ISBN 978-0-670-06334-5 (hardcover)
1. Physical geography—Juvenile literature. 2. Animals—Juvenile literature. I. Title.
GB58.L58 2008        910-dc22        2007040460

Manufactured in China        Set in Typeka        Book design by Nancy Brennan